KT-498-738

EMMA CHICHESTER CLARK

AMAZING MR ZOOTY!

Andersen Press • London

Mr Zooty was out and about on the lookout. He looked out for people to help out. "Get out, help out," was his motto, and he liked it.

He was watching Lucy and Sam
Taylor who were trying to
catch leaves for luck.
They'd been trying
for ages.

"How many have we got?"
asked Sam.

"Only three," said Lucy.
"But three is better
than nothing."

Mr Zooty
watched them giving
the leaves to their mother.
"Well done!" she said.
"We could do with some luck."

"I thought so," said Mr Zooty.
He looked in his little red case.
"Aha!" he said. "Now, let's see…"

Mr Zooty hobbled towards
the Taylors.
"Spare a penny for a poor old cat?"
They looked at him sadly.
"I wish we could,"
said Mrs Taylor, "but
we have nothing."

"Wait!" cried Lucy.
"Have these lucky leaves.
You look like you need them
even more than we do."

Mr Zooty put them
in his little red case
and said thank you.

But as he was going away,
he suddenly swooned...

...and fainted.

"Oh! The poor thing!"
said Mrs Taylor.
"We must help him."

"What are we going
to do with him?" asked Lucy.
"We'll help him get back on his feet," said Mrs Taylor.
"Why?" asked Sam.
"Because everybody needs
a little help sometimes," said Mrs Taylor.

Mrs Taylor pulled Mr Zooty
up the stairs to their little flat.
When they got to the top,
suddenly…

...Mr Zooty leapt out of the chair
and threw off his tattered coat.
"That's enough!" he said.
"Now it's my turn to help you."

He looked in his
little red case.
"Aha!" he said.

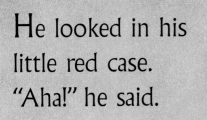

He held up the
lucky leaves.
"Everyone close your
eyes and each make one wish."

"*Pancakes!*" cried Sam.
"That was *my* wish!"
"And maple syrup!" said Mr Zooty.
"That was *my* idea!"

"Now for the second wish," said Mr Zooty.
He looked in his little red case.
"Aha!" he said. Out came a ruby red purse.
He gave it to Mrs Taylor.
"This is for you," he said.
"It means no more worrying!

And..." said Mr Zooty...

"...a lovely new hat! That was *my* idea!"

"Now it's Lucy's wish," said Mr Zooty. "Can you all choose one favourite thing."

"Ready?" asked Mr Zooty.
"Ready!" said the Taylors.
"Did you wish for a balloon?"
asked Mrs Taylor.
"No…" said Lucy.

"We're going to find my wish,
aren't we, Mr Zooty?"
"Yes," said Mr Zooty.
He looked in his little red case.
"Aha!" said Mr Zooty.
Out came a compass,
which Mr Zooty examined.
"25 degrees West,
2 degrees North.
Soon be time for breakfast!"

"Are we there yet?"
asked Sam.
"Nearly!"
said Mr Zooty.

He looked in his little red case.
"Aha!" he said. "Muffins and jam!"
"Did you wish for a picnic?" asked Mrs Taylor.
"No," said Lucy.
"Are we nearly there, Mr Zooty?"

"This way!" said Mr Zooty.
"Follow me!"

"Did you wish for a boat?" asked Mrs Taylor.
"No," said Lucy. "I wished for…"
"Shh! Don't tell!" said Mr Zooty.

Mr Zooty tied the boat up.

Then he looked in
his little red case.
"Aha!" said Lucy,
before Mr Zooty.
Mr Zooty held up
a golden key.

It opened a gate at the end of a path.
"Here we are!" said Mr Zooty. "Lucy's wish."
"A kitten!" cried Lucy.
"And a *garden!*" said Mr Zooty.

"*And a house . . .*"
whispered Mrs Taylor.
"I kept having ideas..."
said Mr Zooty.
"But if you don't want it..."
"How can we ever thank you?"
asked Mrs Taylor.

"You don't need
to thank me,"
said Mr Zooty.
"Everybody needs a
little help sometimes!"
He got back into his boat
and waved goodbye,
as he sailed away
down the river.

PORTSMOUTH CITY COUNCIL
LIBRARY SERVICE

WITHDRAWN

CL-3

C800486943